Springtime Crime

Nancy Drew

* CLUE BOOK *

#9

Springtime Crime

BY CAROLYN KEENE * ILLUSTRATED BY PETER FRANCIS

Aladdin

NEW YORK   LONDON   TORONTO   SYDNEY   NEW DELHI

This book is a work of fiction. Any references to historical events, real people, or real places are used fictitiously. Other names, characters, places, and events are products of the author's imagination, and any resemblance to actual events or places or persons, living or dead, is entirely coincidental.

ALADDIN

An imprint of Simon & Schuster Children's Publishing Division
1230 Avenue of the Americas, New York, New York 10020
First Aladdin paperback edition March 2018
Text copyright © 2018 by Simon & Schuster, Inc.
Illustrations copyright © 2018 by Peter Francis
Also available in an Aladdin hardcover edition.
ALADDIN and related logo are registered trademarks of Simon & Schuster, Inc.
NANCY DREW, NANCY DREW CLUE BOOK, and colophons
are registered trademarks of Simon & Schuster, Inc.
All rights reserved, including the right of reproduction in whole or in part in any form.
For information about special discounts for bulk purchases, please contact Simon & Schuster
Special Sales at 1-866-506-1949 or business@simonandschuster.com.
The Simon & Schuster Speakers Bureau can bring authors to your live event.
For more information or to book an event contact the Simon & Schuster Speakers Bureau
at 1-866-248-3049 or visit our website at www.simonspeakers.com.
Series designed by Karina Granda
Cover designed by Nina Simoneaux
Interior designed by Tom Daly
The illustrations for this book were rendered digitally.
The text of this book was set in Adobe Garamond Pro.
Manufactured in the United States of America 0218 OFF
2 4 6 8 10 9 7 5 3 1
Library of Congress Cataloging-in-Publication Data
Names: Keene, Carolyn, author. | Francis, Peter, 1973- illustrator. Title: Springtime crime / by
Carolyn Keene ; illustrated by Peter Francis. Description: First Aladdin hardcover/paperback
edition. | New York : Aladdin, 2018. | Series: Nancy Drew clue book ; #9 | Summary: Nancy and
her Clue Crew meet Miss LaLa, a superstar who grew up in River Heights, and investigate what
happened to the special hat she ordered for her concert at the annual Flower Sculpture contest.
Identifiers: LCCN 2017018003 | ISBN 9781481499545 (hc) | ISBN 9781481499538 (pbk)
Subjects: | CYAC: Singers—Fiction. | Hats—Fiction. | Flowers—Fiction. | Mystery and detective
stories. | BISAC: JUVENILE FICTION / Mysteries & Detective Stories. | JUVENILE FICTION /
Social Issues / Friendship. | JUVENILE FICTION / Readers / Chapter Books.
Classification: LCC PZ7.K23 Spr 2018 | DDC [Fic]—dc23
LC record available at https://lccn.loc.gov/2017018003
ISBN 9781481499552 (eBook)

✴ CONTENTS ✴

Chapter

1

FLOWER POWER

"Today spring finally feels like spring!" eight-year-old Nancy Drew declared.

It was Friday afternoon and the first mild day of the year. After months of woolly hats, warm scarves, and puffy parkas, Nancy and her two best friends were wearing spring jackets in ice-cream colors.

"It's starting to look like spring too!" Bess Marvin pointed out. "Look at all the pretty flowers."

"Not just flowers, Bess," George said. "Flower *sculptures*!"

Nancy took a whiff of the awesome-smelling statues and sculptures made from fresh flowers. The temperature-controlled greenhouse they stood inside was the perfect place for the first annual River Heights Flower Sculpture Show.

"Why are all the flowers pink and white?" Bess wondered. "And round and puffy like ice-skate pom-poms?"

"They're peonies," Nancy replied. "That's the official flower of the show. All the sculptors were told to work with them this year."

"More like pee-*yew*-nees," George said with a frown. "Our next-door neighbors, the Baxters, grow so many that they hang over the fence into our yard!"

"Peonies are so pretty, George," Nancy said. "Why don't you like them?"

"Because bees like them too!" George complained.

Nancy, Bess, and George strolled through the

greenhouse. The flower show was on Sunday but people were welcome to watch the sculptors put the finishing touches on their sculptures.

"I like that one best!" Bess said, pointing to a peony sculpture of a high-heeled shoe.

"No way." George shook her head. "The peony robot is the best."

"High-heeled shoe? Robot?" Nancy teased. "Are you sure you're related?"

Bess and George traded smiles. Not only did the two cousins look different—Bess had blond hair and blue eyes, while George had dark hair

and dark eyes—they liked different things too. Bess loved girly-girl clothes and accessories. George loved accessories too—as long as they went with her computer and electronic gadgets.

"If you were making a flower sculpture, Nancy," Bess asked, "what would it be of?"

"My clue book!" Nancy replied right away.

Bess and George nodded their approval. The three friends were the Clue Crew, the best kid detectives in River Heights. To help solve their mysteries, Nancy used a clue book to write down their thoughts, clues, and suspects.

"These sculptures are totally neat," George admitted, "but the best part of the show on Sunday will be seeing—"

"Miss LaLa!" Bess cut in. "I still can't believe our favorite singer will be the star of the flower sculpture show on Sunday!"

"I already met Miss LaLa," George said. "My mom catered her after-concert party here in River Heights a year ago. Did I ever tell you that?"

"About a hundred times, George," Bess

groaned. "You told us she dressed up like a cater-
pillar inside a cocoon."

Nancy giggled. Miss LaLa was known for her
beautiful violet eyes—and her wild costumes!

"I heard that Miss LaLa will wear a huge hat
to the flower show," Nancy said excitedly, "totally
covered in peonies!"

"Peonies again?" George sighed. "I hope there
are no bees in her bonnet."

"Or in that flower cupcake," Bess declared.

Nancy looked to see where Bess was pointing.
She smiled when she saw a giant white cupcake
made of peonies.

Standing on a ladder while sticking a pink
peony onto the top was a kid the girls recognized
at once.

"Hey, it's Benjamin Bing," Nancy said.

"It's him, all right," George agreed. "Who else
would sculpt a giant cupcake?"

Ben's parents owned a health food and flower
store on Main Street called Bing's Buds and Bran.

"Is it true that no sweets are allowed in Ben's

house?" Bess whispered. "Only food from his parents' healthy store?"

Nancy nodded yes. "No wonder Ben likes to sculpt what he can't eat," she said. "Cookies, cakes, cupcakes—"

"Don't forget doughnuts," Ben said, climbing down from the ladder. "I sculpt those, too."

Nancy was embarrassed that Ben had heard them talking about him. "We were also saying how awesome your flower cupcake is, Ben," she said quickly.

"Yeah," George agreed. "It looks like the cupcakes my mom just put on the windowsill to cool."

Ben's eyes grew wide. "Cupcakes?"

"My mom's a caterer," George explained. "She has a special catering kitchen in a trailer behind our house."

"Buttercream frosting? Marshmallow?" Ben demanded to know. "Do the cupcakes have sprinkles?"

Nancy tried to change the subject. "How will

you keep your flowers fresh until Sunday, Ben?" she blurted.

"Hair spray," Ben said matter-of-factly.

"Hair spray?" Bess asked, surprised. "For flowers?"

"Watch and learn," Ben said. He pulled out an aerosol can and held it a few inches from the fluffy white peonies. Then Ben turned to the girls, spraying as he explained. "Hair spray isn't just for hairstyles anymore. One good spritz will keep your flowers from wilting and even keep the dust off!"

Nancy, Bess, and George stared open-mouthed at Ben's sculpture as he kept spraying and talking. Something . . . was not . . . right. . . .

"Not only that," Ben went on, "clear hair spray will keep flowers nice and firm—"

"Um . . . Ben?" Nancy interrupted.

George formed a T with her hands. "Time out for a second."

"Why?" Ben asked, still spraying away.

"Since when is clear hair spray brown?" Bess asked.

"Huh?" Ben said. He turned to look at his sculpture and gasped. A whole side of his snowy-white cupcake was now brown!

Ben stopped spraying at once. He looked at the can and began to wail. "Arrrgh! This isn't hair spray. It's brown hair dye!"

"It's okay, Ben," Nancy said gently. "Just pluck

out the brown ones and replace them with white ones."

"I can't!" Ben cried, pointing to his sculpture. "These are the last peonies from my parents' greenhouse!"

The girls left Ben pacing nervously by his sculpture. Nancy felt bad for him and wanted to help. But how?

"Maybe he could spray-paint them white," George suggested.

"I don't think that would look very good. What about . . ." Bess trailed off midthought.

"I may have an idea!" Nancy squeaked.

The three of them had stopped in front of a giant poodle sculpture made of snow-white peonies. In River Heights there was only one sculptor famous for his peony poodles. He was from France and his name was Monsieur Pierre.

"If Pierre uses peonies for his sculptures," Nancy said hopefully, "maybe he has some extras for Ben."

Bess nodded her approval. "Let's ask him!"

But where was Monsieur Pierre? Nancy was about to ask another sculptor, when they heard voices. Angry voices coming from behind the peony poodle.

The girls peeked around the sculpture to see Monsieur Pierre arguing with Mayor Strong.

"I was told I'd be the star of the flower show on Sunday," Pierre said. "How dare you ask Miss LuLu instead?"

"It's 'LaLa,' and we're lucky she'll be singing at the flower show," Mayor Strong said. "Her white peony hat came all the way from Paris, you know."

"Well, so did I!" Pierre scoffed. "And my two poodles, Céline and Celeste!"

Nancy had heard the names Céline and Celeste before. They were Pierre's standard poodles and the models for his sculptures.

"This isn't a good time, you guys," Nancy whispered. "Let's ask another sculptor for peonies."

But as the girls turned to leave . . .

"Girls!" a hushed voice said. "May I speak with you?"

Nancy's eyes widened at the sight of the woman standing behind them. She wore a black trench coat with huge padded shoulders, dark cat-eye sunglasses, and fire-engine-red lipstick. Her blond hair was tied in a low bun, and she was holding a large brown paper shopping bag.

"Um . . . do we know you?" Nancy asked.

"I think you do," the woman said. She lowered her sunglasses to reveal the deepest violet-blue eyes.

Nancy, Bess, and George gasped. Only one person in the world had eyes like that. It was—

"Miss LaLa!" Nancy cried. "Omigosh!"

Chapter

SCENT-ER STAGE

"Omigosh is right!" Bess squeaked as the famous celebrity slipped her shades back on. "I can't believe it's you, Miss LaLa!"

"We thought you were singing on Sunday," George said. "That's when the flower show is."

LaLa opened her mouth to answer, but instead sneezed so hard the girls jumped back.

"Here, Miss LaLa," Nancy said, handing her a tissue from her pocket. "It's clean."

"Thanks," LaLa said, lowering her voice.

"Now, it's a secret that I'm here today . . . because I need a big favor."

"A favor?" Nancy asked. "From us?"

LaLa nodded, then looked at George. "Your mother is Louise Fayne, the caterer? And your name is Georgia, right?"

George gritted her teeth. She hated her real name more than glitter nail polish and stuffed unicorns. But before she could tell Miss LaLa to call her George—

"Right!" Nancy and Bess chorused.

"I remember you from my after-concert party a year ago, Georgia," LaLa said. "That was right before I became a super-famous star."

"Tell us about the favor, Miss LaLa!" Bess begged.

Miss LaLa lifted

the bag. "In this bag is the hat I'll be wearing to the show on Sunday," she whispered.

The girls peeked inside. Through delicate white paper they could see a bed of white peonies. Miss LaLa's hat!

"I need to keep the flowers fresh inside a refrigerator until Sunday," Miss LaLa explained. "The fridge in my hotel room is too small for such a big hat."

"So you want my mom to keep it in her superbig fridge, the one in her catering kitchen?" George asked.

"I knew she'd have a giant fridge!" Miss LaLa said happily. "Do you think it would be okay with your mom?"

Before George could answer, Bess grabbed the bag. "Louise Fayne is my aunt," she said. "I'm sure she'll say yes."

"Thank you!" Miss LaLa said. "Now, only you girls have seen my hat so far. I want it to be a big surprise on Sunday."

Miss LaLa then threw her head way back.

Nancy, Bess, and George braced themselves for another *ah-chooo!*

"Gesundheit!" a voice said.

Nancy caught a whiff of roses as they turned to see who had spoken. Standing behind them was a woman the girls had met before.

"Hey, aren't you Madame Withers, the perfume lady?" George asked.

"We went on a class trip to your perfume factory a few weeks ago," Nancy added. "You showed us how you make perfumes out of wilted flowers."

"Like Droopy Daffodil, Wilting Wisteria, and Saggy Sunflower!" Bess said excitedly.

"Correct!" Madame Withers said, wafting her scent through the air with one hand. "And today I'm wearing my latest scent, Rotting Roses."

With a grin, Madame Withers held up a fancy glass perfume bottle. "I've also created a new scent just for Miss LaLa," she said. "It's called LaLa's Limpy Lavender."

"Limpy . . . Lavender?" Miss LaLa repeated, not smiling.

"I was hoping you'd wear my perfume on Sunday to spread the word," Madame Withers said. "Or in this case—the smell!"

Madame Withers sprayed the air with Limpy Lavender while—*ah-choo!*—Miss LaLa sprayed the air with another sneeze.

"I think your perfumes are making me sneeze," Miss LaLa told Madame Withers. "And I don't really like dead flowers."

"Dead?" Madame Withers gasped.

"Miss LaLa likes fresh flowers like the ones on her peony hat," Bess said, pointing inside the bag. "We're going to keep them nice and fresh inside George's fridge—"

George's hand clapped over Bess's mouth, but it was already too late. Madame Withers was staring into the bag.

"I seeeee," Madame Withers said softly. "Well, that gives me an idea."

Nancy watched Madame Withers breeze away. What idea did she mean? A new perfume, maybe? Nancy's thoughts were interrupted when

Miss LaLa said, "Thanks again, girls. I'll be at your house Sunday morning at eleven to pick up my hat."

George told LaLa her address. With another big sneeze, the singing star left the greenhouse.

"Miss LaLa asked us to do her a favor!" Bess placed the bag on the floor to high-five Nancy and George with both hands. "How awesome is that?"

"Totally," Nancy agreed. She turned to George and asked, "Will your mom have enough room in her fridge for Miss LaLa's big hat?"

George nodded. "I stuck my project for the school science fair in the fridge this morning. There was lots of room."

"What is your science project, George?" Nancy asked.

"I want to prove that one rotten apple spoils the whole bunch," George explained.

"Rotten apple?" Bess said as she wrinkled her nose. "Can't wait."

"And I can't wait to do Miss LaLa a favor,"

Nancy said. She grabbed the handle of the shopping bag to lift it. "I'll carry the bag to George's house."

"No, me," George said, also taking the handle. "It's my mom's refrigerator—"

"Yes, but I took the bag first," Bess said, also taking hold of the handle. "So let me carry it, please."

Now all three girls were tugging the same handle of Miss LaLa's bag, until . . . *RIIIIIIP!* . . . the whole bag tore in half!

Nancy, Bess, and George watched in horror as Miss LaLa's snowy-white peony hat tumbled onto the floor.

"Oh, no! Miss LaLa's hat!" Nancy cried.

Quickly picking it up, Nancy carefully turned it in her hands. "Luckily it's not dirty," she said. "The petals are still fluffy too."

After giving the petals a soft brush with her hand, Nancy looked up. Everyone—including Monsieur Pierre—was staring at her and Miss LaLa's hat!

"Uh-oh," Nancy gulped.

"LaLa didn't want anybody but us to see her hat," George whispered. "Now everyone here saw it."

"What are we going to do, Nancy?" Bess whispered.

Nancy carefully rewrapped the hat. "Let's be happy LaLa's hat wasn't ruined," she said. "That's what's most important."

It was Nancy who carried the hat four blocks to the Fayne house. All three girls had the same rule: They could walk anywhere as long as it was less than five blocks and as long as they were together. Nancy, Bess, and George didn't mind. They wanted to be together anyway.

"I smell something yummy," Bess said as they filed into Mrs. Fayne's kitchen.

The special catering kitchen was inside a trailer right behind the house. Mrs. Fayne was just pulling a pan of flower-shaped cookies out of the oven. Nancy could see a pan of yellow-and-green-frosted cupcakes cooling on a nearby windowsill.

"The cookies are for the flower show on Sunday," Mrs. Fayne said proudly. "So are the cupcakes."

Mrs. Fayne placed the cookie sheet on the butcher-block table. "Now I have to get to the supermarket," she said. "I just ran out of rainbow sprinkles."

"Ask her about the favor, George," Bess whispered loudly.

"What favor?" Mrs. Fayne asked.

"Miss LaLa asked us to keep her flowered hat in your refrigerator," George said, nodding at the hat in Nancy's arms. "She needs to keep it fresh for the flower show."

"Is it okay, Mrs. Fayne?" Nancy asked.

"It's fine with me," Mrs. Fayne said with a smile. "Miss LaLa was very nice when we met. I'm happy to help." She headed toward the door. "Be sure to lock up when you leave."

"I will, Mom, thanks," George said, holding up the key she kept in her jeans pocket.

Mrs. Fayne left the trailer. Nancy, Bess, and

George walked together to the shiny industrial-size refrigerator.

Opening the door George said, "All systems go!"

Bess reached in, making room on one of the shelves. "All clear," she reported.

Feeling a cold blast from the fridge, Nancy leaned in and placed the hat on a clear shelf. "Done!" she declared.

George shut the fridge door and the girls high-fived.

"Hats off to us!" Bess cheered.

"Miss LaLa won't be here until Sunday," George said. "What should we do tomorrow?"

"Let's go back to the botanical gardens," Bess said. "They're opening the tropical rain forest exhibit tomorrow. I heard they'll have real birds and animals inside."

"And real tropical bugs!" George added.

"Bugs?" Bess gulped. "Let's do something else."

Nancy had an idea. "Let's just listen to LaLa's

music on Saturday," she said, "and get excited about seeing her again—on Sunday!"

"What kind of flowers are those, Hannah?" Nancy asked. "They're such a pretty pink."

It was Saturday morning. Hannah Gruen had placed a vase of flowers on the kitchen table after breakfast. Even Nancy's Labrador puppy, Chocolate Chip, seemed to like them. She was wagging her tail.

"They're carnations," Hannah replied. "A friend in my gardening club dropped them off this morning."

Hannah had been the Drews' housekeeper since Nancy was only three years old. She made the best chocolate chip pancakes, helped Nancy with her homework, and gave the best hugs. To Nancy, Hannah was just like a mother—especially when she reminded her to clean her room.

"Speaking of flowers, Hannah," Nancy said, "Miss LaLa asked George to keep her flowered hat in the catering refrigerator."

"I hope no one eats it," a voice called from the other room.

Nancy turned to see her father walking into the kitchen. "Hannah just put out carnations, Daddy," she said. "Don't they look nice?"

"Sure," Mr. Drew agreed. He tapped his chin thoughtfully. "It just needs a little something extra."

Mr. Drew looked around the kitchen. There was a bowl filled with apples, oranges, and grapes on the counter. He grabbed the colorful arrangement and placed it next to the vase. "There!" he said. "A masterpiece!"

Chip barked her approval and Nancy smiled.

"Awesome, Daddy," Nancy said. "You're not just a lawyer—you're an artist, too!"

She was about to grab an orange from the bowl, when the kitchen phone rang. The ID read *Fayne*.

"It's George. I'll get it," Nancy said. She picked up the phone, but before she could say hi—

"Nancy, you and Bess have got to come over to my mom's kitchen," George's frantic voice said. "Right away!"

Chapter

3

GLOOM IN BLOOM

"Hurry, Nancy," Bess said.

"I'm hurrying," Nancy said, walking as fast as she could. "George didn't tell me why she was so upset. What do you think is wrong?"

"Maybe her mom ran out of crunchy coconut peanut butter," Bess guessed. "It's her favorite."

"Coconut peanut butter?" Nancy asked as they turned the corner. "I never heard of—"

WHAP!! Nancy and Bess grunted as they crashed into a large plastic bag. They took a step back to see who was carrying it.

"Monsieur Pierre!" Nancy exclaimed.

The bag had felt as soft as a pillow, and Nancy could see why. Several flower petals were spilling out from the top. Fluffy white flower petals.

"Are those peony petals?" Bess asked.

"I *do* sculpt peony poodles," Pierre mumbled.

He picked up the bag tie that had fallen off and quickly twisted it back on. He hugged the big plastic garbage bag to his chest and huffed away, saying, *"Au revoir!"*

Nancy and Bess watched Pierre rush down the block.

"Oh, well," Bess said, "I guess he needed more petals for his poodles."

The girls hurried up the block to George's house.

But as they turned in to her front yard, they saw more peony petals on the ground. They seemed to form a trail leading toward the back.

"Could Pierre have come from George's yard?" Nancy wondered out loud.

"It doesn't matter, Nancy," Bess replied. "We're here to see what's up with George, not Pierre."

The two friends walked around the house to where the kitchen trailer stood. Inside, they found George standing near the door. She was wearing Miss LaLa's hat—and a huge frown.

"Omigosh!" Nancy said when she saw the hat. "What happened to Miss LaLa's hat?"

"The flowers were all white and fluffy," Bess said. "Now most are . . . brown and droopy. What's going on?"

"I came into the kitchen this morning to check on the hat," George explained, "and when I opened the fridge and took off the cover—the hat looked like this!"

"I don't get it," Nancy said. "The cold was supposed to keep the flowers fresh."

"Maybe the fridge wasn't cold enough," Bess said.

"It was cold yesterday when we opened it," Nancy said. "Maybe the refrigerator plug fell out?"

Nancy, Bess, and George rushed to the side of the fridge. The cord was plugged firmly into the wall socket.

"Any other ideas?" George sighed.

"Maybe there was a blackout last night," Bess suggested. "That would have turned off the fridge until the blackout was over."

"I know a way to find out," Nancy said. She opened the fridge, then the freezer door. In it was a large container of vanilla ice cream.

"You want to eat ice cream now?" Bess asked with a smile. "Great idea, Nancy!"

Nancy shook her head and said, "I want to *check out* the ice cream."

She lifted the lid and peered inside. The ice cream was solidly packed with a smooth surface.

"When ice cream melts and freezes again, it looks warped," Nancy pointed out. "This ice cream looks fine."

"And yummy!" Bess exclaimed. "What are we waiting for? Let's dig in!"

"Let's not," George said. She took the container from Nancy and placed it back in the fridge. "That ice cream is for my mom's catering job."

"We have a job too," Nancy said. "To figure out how fluffy white peony petals could turn brown so fast."

"This might be a stretch," George said as she placed the hat on the table, "but maybe somebody switched the fresh flowers on the hat with wilted ones."

"Switched?" Nancy said. "Someone would have had to sneak into the kitchen to do that."

"And how could that happen?" Bess asked.

"Because," George shouted, waving her arms, "I forgot to lock the kitchen door yesterday— that's how!"

Nancy and Bess stared at George.

"You know, I can't remember if you locked the door or not," Nancy said.

"Me either. We were too busy talking about Miss LaLa and saying goodbye," Bess agreed.

"I know I forgot," George groaned. "When I got to the kitchen this morning, the door was unlocked."

"Maybe your mom unlocked it," Nancy suggested.

George shook her head. "She never leaves the kitchen without locking it," she said. "Ever."

"And I never leave my house without this," Nancy said, pulling a small book from her jacket pocket. "Ever!"

"Your clue book!" Bess said with a smile.

"You mean this is a mystery?" George asked.

Nancy nodded. "If someone did sneak in to

ruin Miss LaLa's hat, the Clue Crew will find out whodunit."

She opened her clue book to a clean page. Tucked inside was a new pen with purple ink. Nancy used it to write on the top of the page: *Who Did the Switcheroo?*

To figure out who could have done it, the girls first had to figure out a timeline.

"If somebody did sneak into the kitchen," Nancy asked, "what time do you think it happened?"

"It must have been late last night or early this morning," George said. "That's when my family and I were inside the house."

Nancy was about to write, when something suddenly clicked.

"George!" she said. "On the way here, Bess and I saw Monsieur Pierre carrying a huge bag of peonies!"

"He sculpts peony poodles," George said with a shrug. "So what?"

"We found a trail of white peony petals in your yard," Nancy explained. "They went through your backyard to the trailer."

"Monsieur Pierre was mad at Miss LaLa," Bess said, "for being the star of the flower show on Sunday. Maybe he ruined her hat on purpose."

But George shook her head. "I've been inside the kitchen for almost an hour," she said. "If Monsieur Pierre was in here, I think I would have known it!"

"Unless he hid outside after the switcheroo," Bess suggested, "waiting for a good time to make a run for it."

"Pierre also saw us drop Miss LaLa's hat yesterday," Nancy added. "So he knows we have it."

George shrugged again. "Okay, okay," she said, "I guess Pierre is our first suspect."

Nancy wrote Pierre's name on her suspect list. She tapped her pen on the notebook, lost in her thoughts.

"What's that smell?" Nancy asked suddenly, sniffing the air. "It smells like flowers."

"The peonies on the hat?" Bess guessed.

"No," Nancy said, looking around the room, "I smell roses. And I know the smell of roses—Hannah's garden is full of them."

"No roses in here," George said. She nodded at the hat on the table. "Just a bunch of wilted peonies."

Wilted? The word made Nancy's eyes light up.

"You guys, I think I smell more than just roses," Nancy declared. "I smell trouble!"

Chapter

4

NOSE FOR A ROSE

"Trouble?" Bess asked. "I thought you said you smelled roses, Nancy."

"I did," Nancy said. "Yesterday Madame Withers was wearing a perfume called Rotten Roses. And we know she has all kinds of wilted flower petals in her perfume factory."

"Maybe wilted peony petals!" Bess gasped.

"Why would Madame Withers want to switch the fresh flowers with her wilted ones?" George asked.

"Remember how angry Madame Withers was when Miss LaLa wouldn't wear her perfume?" Nancy asked. "She saw LaLa's hat in the bag and knew we were taking it here too."

"Thanks to Bess," George muttered.

Bess gave George a look as Nancy remembered something else.

"We heard Madame Withers say she had an idea," Nancy reminded them. "Maybe the idea was to ruin Miss LaLa's hat."

"Okay," George said, "but how do we know Madame Withers has wilted peony flowers in her factory too?"

Nancy knew there was only one way to find out.

"Let's take another field trip," Nancy said after adding Madame Withers's name to her suspect list. "To the perfume factory."

George made sure to lock the door when the girls left the kitchen trailer. They knew exactly where to find the factory. It was on Main Street, right above a cool new all-day pizza parlor called 24-Hour Pizza.

"I heard they have a chocolate pizza," Bess said excitedly, "with mini marshmallows!"

Suddenly the door to the adjoining building swung open. The girls stared wide-eyed when they saw who stepped out.

"It's Madame Withers!" George hissed.

Yawning, Madame Withers didn't seem to notice the girls as she began walking away up the block.

"She looked so sleepy," Bess pointed out.

"It's proof!" George exclaimed. "She was up all night switching fresh peonies with rotten ones!"

Nancy looked up to the window of Madame Withers's perfume factory. She knew it was on the second floor.

"That's not really enough evidence, George. Let's go upstairs and look for wilted peonies," Nancy suggested.

"But the door is probably locked," George said.

"Unless Madame Withers forgot to lock the door." Bess gave George a sideways glance. "Like somebody else I know."

"Ha-ha," George said sarcastically. "Very funny!"

Nancy, Bess, and George entered the building. They filed up a staircase leading to the factory and approached the door.

"It's unlocked," George said, opening the door. "Are we lucky or what?"

But when Nancy, Bess, and George walked into the factory, they saw they were not alone. A man sat behind a front desk. He had a short beard and curly hair. His nameplate read LANCE RIVERS.

"Hi," Nancy said nicely. "May we look inside the perfume factory?"

"Sorry, girls," Lance said. "We don't give tours of Madame Withers's perfume factory on Saturdays."

The girls traded worried looks. How would they get into the factory now?

"Um . . . we were already on a class trip here," Nancy said. "So—"

"So I left something in the factory," George cut in quickly. "By mistake."

"What did you lose?" Lance asked.

Nancy, Bess, and George traded more looks. They would have to make up something that was lost—and fast!

"Her sneaker!" Bess blurted.

Lance leaned over his desk to look at George's feet. "But she's wearing two sneakers," he said.

"Those are her Saturday sneakers," Nancy said, "not her school trip sneakers."

Lance wrinkled his brow. "How do you lose a sneaker?" he asked.

"Who knows?" George said with a shrug.

"We just know you wouldn't want a stinky sneaker in your perfume factory," Bess said. "Would you?"

"My sneakers don't stink, Bess!" George muttered.

But Lance was already pointing to another door. "We certainly don't want anything stinky near Madame Withers's perfumes," he said. "Go inside but be quick."

"Thank you!" Nancy, Bess, and George said at the same time. They then scooted through the door that led to the perfume factory.

"It looks just like it did on the class trip," Bess said as they looked around.

There were dozens of baskets of dried flower petals. And glass jars of wilting flowers. Against one wall stood the big perfume distiller. It had two large tanks connected by a thick, clear glass tube. That was where the wilted flowers were turned into perfume.

"How do we know which petals are peony?" Bess wondered, checking out the baskets. "They're all brown and droopy."

Nancy was about to join Bess at the baskets, when she spotted a big white screen on one side of the room. What was behind it? She was about to walk toward it when—

"You guys," George called from a shiny white desk, "I just found the most awesome clue!"

"Probably not a good idea to turn on Madame Withers's computer, George," Nancy warned.

"It's not on her computer," George said, holding up a notepad. "My mom's name and address are written right here!"

Nancy hurried to the desk to look at the notepad. Sure enough, Mrs. Fayne's name and address were scribbled on it.

"This is an awesome clue, George!" Nancy exclaimed. "Check it out, Bess!"

But Bess was too busy checking something else out—Madame Withers's perfume distiller.

"Bess, what are you doing?" George asked.

"Trying to remember how this works," Bess said. "Madame Withers told us there's a button somewhere here."

She pointed to a button on the side of the tank. "There it is," she said. But when Bess accidentally tapped it—

WHIRRRRRRRRR!!!

All three girls stood frozen, watching a colored liquid bubbling through the glass tube.

"Oh, no, Bess," Nancy cried. "You turned on the perfume machine!"

"I know!" Bess wailed as a sweet-smelling liquid gushed from a spout onto the floor. "Now how do you turn it off?"

Chapter

5

WILT AND SPILT

"Madame Withers showed us how it turns on," Nancy said. "But she never showed us how it turns off!"

George grabbed a fancy empty perfume bottle and stuck it under the spout. The perfume poured into the bottle but gushed so fast that it filled up in seconds!

"More bottles, you guys!" George demanded.

Nancy and Bess passed glass bottles to George, who filled them up one by one.

"Pee-yew—this stuff stinks!" George complained.

"Girls," a voice said. "Try the switch underneath the red button."

Nancy, Bess, and George froze. It was the voice of Madame Withers.

"Um . . . thanks," Nancy said as she flipped the red switch down. The bubbling and gushing slowed to a stop.

"That wasn't so hard, was it?" Madame Withers asked as the girls turned to face her. Standing beside Madame Withers was Lance—looking very stressed.

"Those girls tricked me, Madame!" Lance cried. "Something about a stinky sneaker!"

"It's okay, Lance, it's okay," Madame Withers said. "Why don't you make a fresh pot of herbal tea and I'll take it from here."

Lance scowled at the girls before huffing out of the room.

"The scent pouring out of the distiller is called Lifeless Laurel," Madame Withers said as she walked toward the filled bottles. "Have you ever smelled anything so nice?"

George folded her arms across her chest and said, "We're actually here to talk to you about some wilted flowers. The peonies on Miss LaLa's hat."

Madame Withers blinked, then said, "Wilted? I thought Miss LaLa said she didn't like wilted flowers."

"She doesn't," Bess said. "Which is why we thought you made the switcheroo."

"Switcheroo?" Madame Withers repeated.

"Fresh white peonies on Miss LaLa's hat were switched with wilted ones," Nancy explained.

"So you thought I switched the flowers," Madame Withers said. "Well, I did nothing of the kind."

"But you said you had an idea!" Bess said.

Madame Withers blinked again. "Who are you girls?" she asked. "Some kind of kid detectives?"

"Yes," Nancy said. "We call ourselves the Clue Crew."

"And we're wicked good," George added.

"Oh, I'll bet you are," Madame Withers said with a smile. "And I did have an idea. Follow me." She led the girls over to the big white screen.

"Ta-da!" Madame Withers sang out after she moved the screen aside. "What do you think?"

Nancy, Bess, and George stared at what was behind the screen: a statue made out of wilted peonies. A statue of a woman wearing a peony hat!

"That's Miss LaLa, isn't it?" Bess asked.

"Correct!" Madame Withers said happily. "I worked all night on it for the flower show tomorrow. If Miss LaLa won't advertise my new perfume, I figured this beautiful flower sculpture could!"

"All night?" Nancy asked. "So you were here in the factory all that time?"

Madame Withers nodded. "So I couldn't have been anywhere else but here," she said. "You detectives call that an alibi, right?"

"Right," Nancy agreed, "but it doesn't explain why George's kitchen smells like rose perfume all of a sudden."

"And why you have my mom's name and address on your desk," George added.

"Your mom is Louise Fayne?" Madame Withers asked. "She catered a party at my perfume store last week. She told me she loved my Rotting Roses scent."

"But she never smells like roses," George said.

"Pickles sometimes," Bess added. "But only when she's making coleslaw."

"She'll smell like roses now," Madame Withers said. "I mailed her a bottle a few days ago, so she must have just gotten it."

Madame Withers pointed to her desk and said, "I looked up your mom's address online and wrote it on the pad."

It made sense to Nancy. But she still had a few questions. Before she could ask them, however, Madame Withers walked over to her newly filled bottles. While she capped them one by one, Nancy whispered to her friends.

"How do we know for sure Madame Withers was here all night? Looking sleepy isn't enough proof."

George began wiggling her nose. "Hey. Do you smell that?" she asked.

"We smell a lot of stuff here," Bess said. "We're in a perfume factory, remember?"

"It's not perfume," George said, still sniffing the air. "I think it's . . . pizza."

Pizza? Nancy's eyes darted around the room, looking for the source of the cheesy smell. She spotted two empty-looking pizza boxes in the corner on the floor. But to Nancy, the boxes were a lot more than pizza!

"You guys," Nancy whispered, "I spy with my little eye—a clue!"

Chapter

6

EYE ON THE PIE

"You mean the pizza boxes?" Bess whispered after following Nancy's gaze.

"I don't smell a clue," George said. "Just two greasy pizza boxes from 24-Hour Pizza—that smell a lot better than perfume, by the way!"

"Shh!" Nancy whispered. She glanced over at Madame Withers. The perfume lady had stopped capping bottles to answer a phone, her back turned to the girls.

"I'm thinking Madame Withers must have

been working all night like she told us," Nancy said softly.

"Why?" Bess asked.

"When we have all-night sleepovers, how many pizzas do we order?" Nancy said.

"Usually two," George replied.

"Cheese and pepperoni," Bess added.

"So if we have two-box pizza sleepovers," Nancy said, "Madame Withers must have had a two-box work-over!"

"Two boxes of pizza for just one person?" Bess asked. "That's a lot even for me."

"Lance might have been helping her," Nancy said. "But how do we know the pizzas are from last night?"

"Let's see if there's a leftover slice inside," George suggested. "If it's warm and gooey, it's from this morning. If it's cold and gunky, it's from last night."

But when the girls opened both boxes, they found something better: two receipts stamped with dates and times. The first pizza had been ordered at midnight—the second at three o'clock in the morning!

"Madame Withers was working all night," Nancy decided. "And eating pizza too!"

Madame Withers ended her call. As she turned to the girls, Nancy said, "We want to apologize for turning on your perfume maker, Madame Withers."

"And help you clean up," Bess offered.

"It's no problem at all," Madame Withers said kindly. "You girls have already helped me in a big, big way."

"How?" Nancy asked.

"By bottling my new perfume!" Madame Withers said, gazing lovingly at their work. "And I think I smell a hit!"

As they headed toward the door, George stopped to ask, "Madame Withers, where do you get so many wilted flowers?"

"Oh, lots of different places. Sometimes I get them from Pierre, the peony poodle sculptor," Madame Withers replied. "When flowers in his studio begin to wilt, he gives them to me."

She pointed to the sculpture of Miss LaLa and said, "Pierre gave me those wilted peonies over a week ago. They sure came in handy."

The girls thanked Madame Withers and Lance before leaving the building.

"Madame Withers just gave us a clue," Nancy pointed out. "Pierre would have lots of wilted flowers. He could have used them to switch the flowers on the hat."

Nancy crossed Madame Withers out of her clue book. Then she added the new clue about Pierre.

"George, I'd like to go back to your house," Nancy said as she shut her clue book, "and see where that trail of peony petals leads."

"Sure," George said. "And while we're there, I'd like to find out something too."

"What?" Nancy asked.

"If my mom really does wear Rotting Roses perfume," George said.

* * *

Most of the peony petals were still on the grass when Nancy, Bess, and George reached the Fayne house. But just as they were about to follow the trail—

WHOOOSH! A sudden gust of wind scattered the peony petals in all different directions!

"There goes our trail." Nancy sighed.

"Gone with the wind." Bess sighed too.

"Hi, girls!" a voice called out.

Nancy, Bess, and George turned to see Mrs. Fayne walking to her catering van in the driveway.

"Where are you going, Mom?" George asked.

"I just have to drive to the bank," Mrs. Fayne answered. "I'll be right back."

"Wait, Mom," George said. "Before you go . . ."

Nancy thought George was going to ask her mother about the rose perfume.

Instead, George took a deep breath and said, "I'm sorry I didn't lock the kitchen door yesterday. I must have been thinking about something else."

"But you did lock the door, George," Mrs. Fayne said.

"I did?" George asked, surprised. "Are you sure?"

Mrs. Fayne nodded and said, "Very early this morning, while you were in bed, I remembered that the cupcakes were still on the windowsill. I went to the trailer to take them down."

As she opened the van door, Mrs. Fayne continued, "After I put the cupcakes on the table, I decided to take out the recycling. My hands were full, so I couldn't lock the door on the way out."

"Didn't you come back to lock it?" George asked.

Shaking her head, Mrs. Fayne said, "I guess I forgot."

"Wow," George said with a smile. "So that's why the door was unlocked this morning."

"My bad!" Mrs. Fayne sighed. "By the way, did any of you eat one of my cupcakes yesterday?"

"No," Nancy, Bess, and George said together.

"Well, that's strange. . . ." Mrs. Fayne trailed off midthought as she climbed into the van. She slid the door shut, then called out the window, "I'll be right back."

As Mrs. Fayne drove off, Bess patted George's shoulder.

"You locked the door yesterday, George," she said happily. "Aren't you glad you found that out?"

"I also found out something else," George said, wrinkling her nose. "That my mom really does wear Rotting Roses perfume. Did you smell that stuff?"

"Yes," Nancy said with a smile. She was glad that George hadn't forgotten to lock the kitchen door. But it brought up another question.

"If the door was locked all night," Nancy said, "how did the peony switcher get inside the trailer?"

The girls headed over to the trailer. George pointed up to the window, still open. "Maybe he or she climbed through there," she suggested.

"What's this thing?" Bess asked.

She picked up a card protected by a clear plastic cover. Attached to it was a clip.

"It looks like someone's photo ID," Nancy said. "It says it's from the botanical gardens."

"Then it might be your mom's, George," Bess said. "She's been working on those parties for the flower show."

"Could be," George said as she pointed to the card. "But since when is my mom's name Benjamin Bing?"

Chapter 7

RAIN FOREST ROMP

"It's Ben's ID card?" Nancy asked. She took the card from Bess and checked it out. Sure enough, the card had his name and picture.

"What would Ben be doing outside my mom's catering kitchen?" George asked. "And right under an open window?"

"It's not like Ben would want to switch the flowers on Miss LaLa's hat," Bess said.

Nancy was about to agree, when she remembered something important. "Maybe Ben wanted to replace the ones he sprayed brown with fresh white ones."

"Ben said the flowers he used were the last from his parents' greenhouse, too," George remembered. "He could have been desperate."

"Ben could have seen the hat fall out of the bag," Bess said. "Almost everybody in the greenhouse did."

"Ben knows where I live, too," George said. "He sent me an invitation to his birthday party when I was about six."

"Was it fun?" Nancy asked.

"If you like spinach and cauliflower birthday cake," George said. She suddenly noticed something a few feet away. "Hey, look at that."

George gestured to a nearby crate. On the top was a kid-size sneaker print. "Ben could have used that to climb up to the window," she said.

Nancy checked out the sneaker print on the crate. All arrows seemed to be pointing to Benjamin Bing!

"Let's go to the botanical gardens right

away," Nancy said, "and talk to Ben."

The girls heard a rumble, and Mrs. Fayne drove up the driveway, back from her errand. She told them her next stop was the botanical gardens, to deliver some baked treats for the flower show the next day.

"I baked too many flower cookies yesterday," Mrs. Fayne said. "So help yourself to some in the kitchen."

"Thanks, Mom," George said. "But can we go with you to the botanical gardens instead?"

"Sure," Mrs. Fayne said. "Any special reason?"

"We have work to do too, Mrs. Fayne," Nancy explained. "Detective work!"

Mrs. Fayne was happy to drive the girls. Nancy, Bess, and George were happy for the ride.

After parking the van, Mrs. Fayne carried baked goods to the botanical gardens' party room. Nancy, Bess, and George made their way toward the greenhouse.

The spring air was filled with the scent of wildflowers. As the girls passed a big white building with a domed roof, they saw Mayor Stone standing in front of the main entrance. He was wearing a fancy black top hat and was speaking to a crowd of people.

"What's going on over there?" George wondered.

"It's probably the opening ceremony for the tropical rain forest exhibit," Nancy said.

"You mean with the tropical bugs?" Bess said with a shiver. "Keep walking."

Nancy, Bess, and George did walk the short distance to the greenhouse. Once inside, they went straight to Ben's cupcake sculpture. They were surprised to find it hidden behind a canvas curtain. A sign pinned to the curtain read UNDER CONSTRUCTION.

"I'll bet Ben is sticking Miss LaLa's fresh white peonies into his sculpture right now," George said angrily. "Why else would he be working in secret?"

Suddenly Ben peeked out from behind the curtain, a temporary ID hanging around his neck. When he saw the girls, his jaw dropped.

"Hi, Ben," Nancy said. "We just want to—"

"I didn't mean it!" Ben cut in. "It was temporary insanity or too much sugar—I mean, quinoa!"

He popped back behind the screen.

"Was that just a confession?" Bess asked.

"I'm not sure," Nancy said.

Ben darted out from behind the curtain and headed toward the exit.

"Stop him!" George cried.

Nancy, Bess, and George squeezed through the crowd of visitors, following Ben.

"I said I didn't mean it!" Ben called back before racing out the door. The girls raced out after him. They chased him through gardens and around fountains and grassy animal topiaries.

Ben kept the lead until the rain forest exhibit blocked his path. Mayor Strong was about to cut a ribbon held across the door by a park ranger and a guy in a parrot suit.

"Thank you, Botanical Gardens," Mayor Strong boomed, "for bringing a real tropical rain forest to River Heights!"

"Raise the roof, raise the roof," squawked the parrot. "Arrrrk!"

The moment Mayor Strong snipped the ribbon, Ben dashed through the entrance.

"Well, now," Mayor Strong chuckled. "Someone can't wait to visit our rain forest."

The mayor did not chuckle as Nancy, Bess,

and George dashed in too. "Okay, what's going on?" he demanded.

The girls rushed through the exhibit, looking for Ben. Not only did it look like a rain forest, with its lush palm trees and exotic flowers, it felt like one too—hot and humid!

"Does anyone see Ben?" Nancy asked.

"Sorry," Bess said, "I'm too busy watching for bugs!"

Real-live tropical birds cawed from trees as the girls searched for their suspect. Suddenly Nancy heard a stomping noise like running feet. Turning, she saw Ben charging across a wooden bridge.

"There he is!" Nancy shouted.

The wooden bridge arched upward. Ben was just making his way to the peak when *SLAM*—he crashed into a ranger running from the other end.

Ben yelped as he fell onto the planks of the bridge. A flurry of colorful round objects began rolling out of his pockets.

"Gumballs and jelly beans!" Bess exclaimed.

"Look out!" George cried as the candy rolled over the bridge in their direction.

Ben lay frozen on the bridge, watching the girls stumble over spinning gumballs. But as the candy rolled to a stop—

"Eee, eee, eeeeeee!"

What was that?

Nancy looked straight up and gasped. Dropping out of the tropical trees were—

"Monkeys!!" Nancy cried.

Chapter

8

OODLES OF POODLES

Nancy had never seen such tiny monkeys. They were practically the size of guinea pigs.

"Whoa!" George cried. "The monkeys are scooping up the candy!"

More chattering monkeys dropped down as Mayor Strong and the ranger raced over.

"Cheese and crackers, Rosalie!" Mayor Strong cried. "I told the director of this exhibit not to have real live monkeys!"

"They're pygmy marmosets, actually," Rosalie

the ranger explained. "The smallest monkeys in the world."

"Small monkeys with huge appetites," Mayor Strong groaned. "Let's remove them before more guests come in."

The mayor turned to the girls and to Ben, who had returned from the bridge. "Sorry, but I think you kids had better go now. We're closing the exhibit until it's monkey-free."

As monkey handlers hurried over to collect

the pygmy marmosets, Ben reached down for a gumball.

"Eww, Ben, don't eat that!" Bess cried. "It was in monkey hands!"

"Yeah, Ben," George said. "What were you thinking?"

"That's the problem!" Ben cried as he dropped the gumball. "When it comes to candy, I can't think of anything else!"

"We thought you only ate food from your parents' health food store," Nancy said. "So why were your pockets filled with candy?"

"All that candy was from Peter Patino's birthday party last week," Ben explained. "My mom and dad never knew I snuck it home."

"So you secretly carry candy around?" Nancy asked.

"Only when I'm not sneaking bites from cookies, cupcakes, or other yummy stuff," Ben admitted.

Nancy had no idea Ben had such a sweet tooth. But they were not there to talk about candy.

"Speaking of sneaky, Ben," Nancy said, reaching into her pocket and pulling out the photo ID, "we found this outside the Faynes' catering kitchen."

"So that's where I lost it," Ben sighed.

"Then you did climb through the window into the kitchen?" Bess asked.

"To replace the fresh peonies on Miss LaLa's hat with the ones you sprayed brown?" Nancy asked.

Ben shook his head. "Wait a minute, wait a minute," he said. "I didn't do any of that stuff."

"But we found your ID under the window," Nancy said.

"Tell us the truth, Ben," Bess urged.

George leaned over to Nancy and Bess. "You guys," she murmured, "I think Ben is telling the truth."

"How do you know?" Nancy whispered.

Instead of answering, George turned to Ben and asked, "Is that the same jacket you wore yesterday?"

Ben nodded and said, "Yes. Why?"

George pointed to a yellow-and-green stain on the front of Ben's jacket and said, "That tells me you weren't at my house for the switcheroo—but the *snackeroo*!"

"Snackeroo?" Nancy repeated.

"What does that mean?" Bess asked.

"My mom's cupcakes on the windowsill had yellow-and-green icing," George explained. "Just like the stain on Ben's jacket."

"Oh, man," Ben groaned under his breath.

"Remember how my mom asked if we ate one of her cupcakes yesterday?" George asked. "She must have meant one of the cupcakes was missing!"

"Ben?" Nancy asked, raising one eyebrow. "Did you sneak up to the window yesterday to grab a cupcake?"

"It was only one cupcake!" Ben insisted. "When George said her mom had some cooling on the windowsill, I had to have one."

Nancy, Bess, and George traded looks. Each of them knew what the others were thinking.

Ben did not switch the peonies on Miss LaLa's hat.

"Can I have my ID back now?" Ben asked.

"As soon as you tell us something else," Nancy said.

"Now what?" Ben sighed.

Nancy smiled and asked, "What did you do with all the peonies you sprayed brown?"

"Follow me!" Ben said, smiling too.

Nancy, Bess and, George followed Ben back to the greenhouse. He pulled open the curtain and—

"Ta-daaa!" Ben sang. "Double chocolate, anyone?"

Ben pointed to an all-brown sculpture. He had sprayed every white flower on it to create a chocolate cupcake!

"Sweet!" Nancy exclaimed. She handed Ben his ID. Then the girls left him to work on his sculpture. Nancy took out her clue book and crossed Ben's name off their suspect list.

"We have only one suspect left," Bess said.

"Pierre the peony poodle sculptor!" George declared.

"Let's find Pierre," Nancy said, shutting her clue book and slipping it into her jacket pocket, "and ask him a few questions."

The girls walked together to Pierre's work area. Instead of one peony poodle sculpture, they found two!

"There was only one yesterday," Bess pointed out.

"The second poodle might be a clue," Nancy said. "It might have been made with peonies from Miss LaLa's hat."

"But where's Pierre?" George wondered.

Another sculptor overheard George. "Monsieur Pierre went home to walk his poodles, Celeste and Céline," she said.

"Does he live far from here?" Nancy asked.

"Not at all," the sculptor said. "His house and studio are only two blocks away, on Willow Street."

"Thank you," Nancy replied. She then told Bess and George, "We're taking a little walk too—straight to Monsieur Pierre's house!"

As the girls walked to Willow Street, Nancy asked, "What kind of questions should we ask Pierre?"

"I have one," George said with a frown. "How did such a big guy fit through my mom's kitchen window?"

Once on Willow Street, they found a huge peony poodle on someone's front lawn. The house had to be Pierre's!

A sign that read STUDIO pointed toward the back. When Nancy, Bess, and George reached the backyard, their mouths dropped open. Standing on the lawn were about a dozen pink-and-white-peony poodles!

"So this is where Pierre works," Nancy said.

"They look so real!" Bess said as they walked around the sculptures. "Especially this one here."

The fluffy white poodle was sculpted in a sitting position on the grass, but when Bess reached out to point to it—

Woof, woof, woof!

Nancy and Bess screamed as the white-peony poodle stood up, wagging its tail.

"It's alive!" George cried. "It's alive!"

Chapter 9

SPOILED ROTTEN

Another peony poodle came to life just as Nancy, Bess, and George were about to run. Now two dogs were barking and running in circles around the girls!

"*Excusez-moi! Excusez-moi!*" a voice called. "What is happening here?"

Nancy glanced beyond the skittish poodles and saw Pierre racing over. Hanging from his hand were two pink, sparkly dog leashes.

"What are you doing to Celeste and Céline?"

Pierre asked as he took hold of the poodles' collars.

"And what were *you* doing sneaking away from my house with a bag of peonies?" George demanded.

"*Pardon?*" Pierre gulped.

"We saw you carrying it, Pierre," Bess said. "You do remember bumping into us, don't you?"

"We also found a trail of white petals in George's yard," Nancy said. "Right after we saw you leave."

Pierre muttered something under his breath, then said, "I did take the peonies."

Nancy, Bess, and George traded excited looks. Had Pierre just confessed to switching the fresh peonies on Miss LaLa's hat with wilted ones?

"Now if you will *excusez-moi*," Pierre said, lifting the leashes, "I have two poodles that need to piddle."

"Wait, please, Pierre," Nancy said. "We just want to know why you did that to Miss LaLa."

"Is it because you're jealous of her?" George asked.

Pierre looked at the girls with surprise. "What do the peonies I took have to do with Miss LaLa?" he asked.

"You just said you took the peonies," Nancy said, confused. "Didn't you?"

"*Oui!*" Pierre agreed. "I needed more peonies to build my second poodle sculpture. So I cut a bunch from the next-door neighbor's bushes."

"My neighbors, the Baxters?" George asked. "You mean the peonies growing over their fence into our yard?"

"I didn't want your neighbors to see me," Pierre told George, "so I cut their peonies from your yard."

Nancy frowned at Pierre. "Cutting other people's flowers without their permission is not okay," she said.

"A big no-no," Bess added.

"I know, I know," Pierre admitted. "So yesterday I called the Baxters to apologize and make it up to them."

"How?" Nancy asked.

"I agreed to create a peony sculpture of their mixed-breed dog, Fester," Pierre said, rolling his eyes. "He's some kind of . . . Jack-a-poo."

"Half poodle, half Jack Russell," George said with a smile. "Fester is a neat dog!"

Pierre began clipping on his dog's leashes. But Nancy still had questions.

"We had reason to think you ruined Miss LaLa's hat," Nancy said. "We heard you tell Mayor Strong that you didn't like her."

"I do now," Pierre said happily as he pulled out his phone. "Miss LaLa needed dogs for a new video she was shooting this morning and guess which ones she picked?"

Pierre held up his phone. The girls watched as he played a video of Miss LaLa singing while walking two white standard poodles!

"Are those Céline and Celeste?" Nancy asked.

Pierre nodded. "They are not just dogs anymore," he said. "They are celebrities just like Monsieur Pierre!"

Suddenly—

Woof, woof, woof!

Céline and Celeste turned and shot toward a tree. Pierre yelped as the two dogs pulled him across the lawn!

"Celebrities who chase squirrels," Nancy giggled.

"Dogs will be dogs!" George laughed.

The girls called thank you to Pierre and left his yard. As they walked up the block, Nancy crossed another name off her suspect list.

"Pierre is innocent," Nancy declared. "And we

have no more suspects. Zero . . . zip . . . zilch."

"What should we do now, Nancy?" Bess asked.

Nancy glanced at her watch. It was time to go home to walk her own dog, Chocolate Chip. It was also getting close to dinnertime, so—

"Maybe we'd better go home," Nancy said.

"Home?" George exclaimed. "But Miss LaLa will be at my house tomorrow morning to pick up her hat!"

"Her wilted hat," Bess added.

Nancy was worried too. She knew time was running out. But she refused to give up.

"I promise to think about the case all night and tomorrow morning," Nancy said. "Until my brain starts to wilt too!"

"Maybe Mr. Fayne snuck into the kitchen Friday night for a midnight snack," Nancy thought out loud, "and forgot to shut the refrigerator door while he finished off some rocky road ice cream!"

Nancy was about to scribble the thought in

her clue book when Mr. Drew said, "Nancy? What are you doing?"

"Hi, Daddy," Nancy said, looking up from her clue book. "I'm still working on my case."

"I can see that," Mr. Drew said with a smile. "How about working on setting the table instead?"

"Big lasagna dinner tonight," Hannah told Nancy. "I could use your help."

"And I could use a brain break," Nancy said as she closed her clue book. She was about to place it on the kitchen table, when she noticed something different.

"What happened to the pretty carnations that were on the table?" Nancy asked. "The ones next to the fruit bowl?"

"I had to throw them away," Hannah admitted. "They got all brown and wilted all of a sudden."

"So soon?" Nancy asked, surprised. "Why?"

"A woman in my gardening club once told me that placing flowers next to fresh fruit will quicken wilting," Hannah explained. "Although I can't remember why."

"Well, what do you know?" Mr. Drew said. "I guess one bad apple really does spoil the whole bunch—of flowers."

Nancy turned to look at her father. Bad apple . . . whole bunch . . . where had she heard those words before?

Her eyes lit up as it suddenly clicked.

"Omigosh!" Nancy gasped. "George's science project!"

Clue Crew—and
YOU!

Can you solve the case of the wilted peony hat? It's your turn to think like the Clue Crew. Or go to the next page to find out!

1. The Clue Crew ruled out Madame Withers, Benjamin Bing, and Monsieur Pierre. Can you think of others who might want to ruin Miss LaLa's hat? Write their names down on a piece of paper.

2. Nancy suddenly remembered George's bad-apple science project in Mrs. Fayne's refrigerator. Why might this be important? Write one or more reasons on a piece of paper.

3. While working on the case, the Clue Crew used their eyes and ears to find clues. At what time did Nancy use her nose? Write it down on a piece of paper.

Chapter 10

PEONY HARMONY

Nancy loved Hannah's lasagna, but all she could think about through dinner was George's science project. She even saved dessert for later, racing upstairs to do research on her computer.

After reading all about fruits, flowers, and wilting petals, Nancy looked down at Chip sitting at her feet.

"Hannah's friend was right," Nancy told her puppy. "When fruit gets very ripe, it lets out a gas that can make flowers wilt."

Without wasting a minute, Nancy got permission to call George.

"Listen, George, this is important," Nancy said into the phone. "Is your rotten apple experiment still in your mom's fridge?"

"Sure," George said. "But why—"

"Take it out right now, please," Nancy cut in.

"Can't," George said. "I was just on my way out to visit my grandmother. My dad is calling me from the door."

Nancy chewed on her lower lip, then said, "Okay. I'll be at your house tomorrow morning with Bess."

"Did you figure out who ruined LaLa's hat?" George asked.

"Not who," Nancy replied. "What!"

The next morning, Nancy and Bess stood along with George inside the kitchen trailer. Mrs. Fayne had left a platter of flower cookies out for the girls to enjoy.

"Yummy!" Bess said, grabbing a cookie and taking a bite. Nancy also took a cookie. George was too confused to snack.

"Can somebody please tell me what's going on?" George asked.

"I don't know either, George," Bess said between cookie chews. "Nancy said she'd tell us both when we got here."

"Well, we're here now," George said. "So go ahead, Nancy. Spill."

Nancy put her cookie aside. "Okay, but first," she told George, "take Miss LaLa's peony hat out of the fridge."

Bess held the fridge door open while George pulled out the flowered hat. Even more white peonies had become brown and droopy!

"So?" George asked after placing the hat on the table.

"Next, take out your rotten-apple science project," Nancy instructed.

George reached way inside the fridge for her

project. But the moment she pulled it out—

"Yuck!" Nancy exclaimed. "All the apples have gone bad."

"They smell bad too," Bess said, scrunching her nose.

"Which means my science project was a success," George said happily. "One rotten apple really does spoil the whole bunch."

She turned to Nancy and asked, "But what does it have to do with Miss LaLa's hat?"

"Here's what I found out," Nancy said. "The gases in the rotten apple spoiled the other apples—but they also spoil certain flowers like peonies!"

"Really?" Bess asked.

"Then nobody did this on purpose?" George asked.

"Nobody but the rotten apple," Nancy replied.

Bess gave a little gasp. "That is so awesome, Nancy," she said. "Now we know what really ruined Miss LaLa's hat!"

Nancy smiled at Bess. But when she looked at George, all she saw was a frown.

"A lot of good this does," George muttered. She pointed to the clock on the wall. "Miss LaLa will be here to pick up her hat in—"

KNOCK! KNOCK! KNOCK!

"Two seconds," Bess said as they turned toward the door. Was that Miss LaLa knocking? There was only one way to find out.

"Um . . . who is it?" George called.

"It's me—LaLa!" Miss LaLa called back. "I hope you don't mind that I'm a bit early."

Nancy, Bess, and George traded frantic looks. In a blink, they rushed to shove the wilted hat into the fridge.

"No problem, Miss LaLa!" George shouted at the door. She then turned to Nancy and hissed, "What are we going to tell her?"

"The truth," Nancy whispered. "We didn't ruin her hat on purpose. It was an accident."

"A scientific accident," Bess whispered.

All three girls walked to the door. Nancy and Bess peeked over George's shoulder as she slowly opened it.

Standing outside was Miss LaLa, dressed in a pink jumpsuit, a giant flower-petal collar around her neck. She lowered her black shades as she smiled at the girls.

"Good morning!" LaLa said. "Your mom told me you guys were in the trailer . . . trailer. . . ."

She threw back her head with a giant *ah-chooo!*

"You'd better take care of that cold," Bess said as LaLa entered the trailer. "You've been sneezing since yesterday."

"It's not a cold," LaLa sniffed. "I found out that I'm totally allergic to something."

"Yesterday you thought it was Madame Withers's perfumes," George said.

"It's not," LaLa said, shaking her head. "Unless Madame Withers had a perfume made from peonies."

"Peonies?" Nancy asked.

"I was making a video with two poodles in a peony garden yesterday and I couldn't stop sneezing between takes," LaLa sighed. "I'm not allergic to dogs, so it must have been the peonies in the garden."

She shrugged and said, "So it looks like I won't be wearing my peony hat to the flower show."

The girls gaped at Miss LaLa. Then—

"You won't?" George exclaimed.

"Are we lucky or what?" Bess cheered—until getting an elbow nudge from Nancy.

"She means, what terrible luck!" Nancy blurted. "Your peony hat was so pretty—"

"Pretty annoying if it makes you sneeze!" George piped in rapidly. "Don't even think of wearing it, LaLa!"

"Oh, I won't, that's for sure," Miss LaLa agreed as she rubbed her nose to stop another sneeze. "But what will I wear to the flower show instead?"

Nancy's eyes darted around the kitchen for an idea. When she spotted Mrs. Fayne's platter of cookies, she smiled.

"How about a hat made of a different kind of flower, Miss LaLa?" Nancy asked. "What about jumbo flower cookies?"

Miss LaLa clasped her hands together and gasped. "A jumbo flower cookie hat is so me!" she exclaimed. "Girlfriend, you are one smart apple!"

Nancy and her friends gulped. A rotten apple was what had caused the problem in the first place, so—

"Miss LaLa?" Nancy asked. "How about 'smart cookie' instead?"

"Who would think we'd have so much fun today?" George asked later that day. "Especially after what happened to Miss LaLa's hat!"

Nancy nodded in agreement. After crafting the coolest jumbo flower cookie hat for Miss LaLa, the girls had joined their favorite singer at the River Heights Flower Sculpture Show.

"Someone was happy to receive all those wilted peonies," Nancy reminded George and Bess.

"Madame Withers!" Bess declared.

The girls gathered with others to watch Miss LaLa perform her latest song. Making sure to stay far from the peony sculptures, LaLa looked great

in her awesome flower cookie hat.

Looking around, Nancy saw Ben standing proudly next to his flowery chocolate cupcake. She also saw Pierre happily watching Celeste and Céline in LaLa's musical number.

But proudest of all was George—of her rotten-apple science project.

"Who knew that one bad apple would spoil the whole bunch *and* flowers!" George shouted over the music. "My science project will totally rock!"

"Don't forget," Nancy told her friends, "the Clue Crew has something down to a science too."

"We do?" Bess asked. "What?"

"What else?" Nancy said with a grin. *"Mysteries!"*

Test your detective skills with even more Clue Book mysteries:

Nancy Drew Clue Book #10: Boo Crew

"Double, double, toil and trouble!" George Fayne declared. Then she wrinkled her nose and said, "Did witches really talk like that?"

"They spoke that way in William Shakespeare's play *Macbeth*," eight-year-old Nancy Drew said. "I'm glad my dad told me about the old play so we can audition as the three witch sisters!"

Nancy's best friend George rolled the big black cauldron up the street. Her other best friend, Bess Marvin, helped Nancy carry a duffel bag filled with witch costumes and awesome brew ingredients.

George blew dark curly bangs out of her eyes. "'Bubble, bubble' sounds better than 'double, double,'" she said. "Why don't we say that instead?"

"We will have a bubbly cauldron of brew," Bess said happily, "thanks to my bottle of strawberry bubble bath!"

"Then bubble, bubble it is!" Nancy said.

If the girls' hands weren't so full, they would have high-fived. The hit show *Twinkling Little Stars* was coming to River Heights to audition kids for their TV talent contest.

"I'm glad the auditions are for their special Halloween show," Nancy said. "We get to dress up two weeks before Halloween!"

"I hope the judges like our brew ingredients," George said, nodding at the cauldron, "toenail of toad, scale of dragon, tooth of giant—hairball of cat!"

"Ewww," Bess cried. "I'm glad all that stuff is fake—it's totally gross."

"Speaking of gross," George said excitedly.

"I'm going with my mom later to see the movie *Zombie Slime Monsters*!"

"*Zombie Slime Monsters*," Nancy repeated. "Is it true the movie theater will serve slime-green popcorn?"

"Only for the special five o'clock show," George said. "Can't wait!"

Bess stuck her tongue out and made gagging sounds. "Slime-green popcorn? I'll stick to crunchy caramel!"

Nancy giggled and said, "Are you sure you're cousins?" You're as different as—"

"Slime-green and caramel popcorn?" George joked.

Bess used both hands to grab the handle of the bag.

"This bag is getting heavy," she said. "Why do we have to drop off our costumes and props today? It's only Friday and the auditions are Saturday and Sunday."

"Everyone auditioning has to, Bess," Nancy said. "It's the contest rules."

The girls were glad to reach the theater where the auditions would be held. The Heights Theater was old-timey but looked brand new with a fresh coat of paint and a shiny gold front door.

"I wonder if we'll meet the judges today," Nancy said as they filed inside.

"I can't believe Lucy O'Toole is one of the judges," George said. "I think she's the funniest comedian and she grew up right here in River Heights."

"And I can't believe the other judge is the actress Cookie Sugarman!" Nancy said. "Can you believe she's only nine years old and supposed to be the sweetest star in Hollywood!"

"Even Cookie's movies are sweet," Bess said. "I saw *The Princess and the Unicorn* three times!"

"*The Princess and the Unicorn*," George scoffed. "That movie was so sweet I had to brush my teeth three times!"

Bess rolled her eyes at George. "Who's the third judge, Nancy?" she asked.

"It's the owner of this theater," Nancy replied. "I think his name is Nathan."

"Who wouldn't want to own this place?" George asked as they looked around the lobby. "It's awesome!"

Plush red velvet chairs and sofas stood on golden-colored carpeting. Covering the walls were posters from long-ago shows.

"It looks like a fairy-tale castle," Bess said, pointing upward. "Even the ceiling is painted blue with white clouds!"

Nancy couldn't believe her eyes either. The old Heights Theater had just reopened after being rebuilt. The *Twinkling Little Stars* auditions would be the first event there in more than seventy years!

"Do you believe this building used to be old and creepy?" Nancy said. "We even thought it was haunted!"

More kids walked by holding costumes and props. One was Quincy Taylor from the girls' third-grade class. Quincy held a mummy costume as he stopped to face the girls.

"Who says this theater still isn't haunted?" Quincy asked them.

"What do you mean, Quincy?" Nancy asked.

"You heard about the curse, didn't you?" Quincy asked. "About a hundred years ago an actress named Nora Westcott starred in a play here. Nora was mad when the director replaced her with a bigger star."

Quincy lowered his voice almost to a whisper. "The director didn't know that Nora was also a witch!"

"We're witches too," Bess said with a smile. "Bubble, bubble, toil and trouble—"

"—Nora was a real witch," Quincy cut in, "and there was trouble all right."

"Trouble?" Bess asked.

"The Heights Theater has been haunted ever since Nora's curse," Quincy answered. "By ghosts and monsters!"

"Not true!" a deep voice said.

The kids turned to see a tall man with dark hair standing behind them.

"I am Nathan Alonso, the owner of this theater," the man said. "The only thing that ever went bump in the night was when a clumsy stagehand dropped a set piece."

"So there are no ghosts or monsters?" George asked.

"Zero, zip," Nathan insisted. "Zilch."

Quincy smiled. "You've got to be right, Mr. Alonso," he said. "No ghosts or monsters here. Whew, what a relief!"

Nathan walked away. The girls turned to Quincy with surprise.

"What made you change your mind so fast, Quincy?" George asked. "Because he's the owner of the theater?"

"Because he's one of the judges and I want to win!" Quincy said. "Hey, I may be a mummy but I'm no dummy!"

As Quincy walked away, Bess turned to Nancy and George, her blue eyes wide.

"What if Quincy's right?" Bess asked. "What if this theater is filled with monsters and ghosts?"

"Quincy is always talking about ghosts," George scoffed. "He's a member of that goofy Ghost Grabbers Club."

Bess nodded. "Yes, remember when they tried to help us solve the mystery of Murray the Monster Mutt?" she sighed. "They weren't much help."

"Who cares about grabbing ghosts?" Nancy asked with a smile. "I like our own club, the Clue Crew!"

As the Clue Crew, Nancy, Bess, and George solved mysteries all over River Heights. Nancy even owned a clue book where she wrote down all of their suspects and clues.

"Quincy can look for ghosts if he wants to," George said as she rolled the cauldron. "I want to find the prop room so I can park this pot!"

Nancy, Bess, and George followed the others down a hall to a large room. Inside, kids were busy hanging up costumes and placing props on shelves.

"There's Shelby!" George said, pointing to

their friend Shelby Metcalf from school. "She's juggling monster eyeballs!"

A few feet away was another kid wearing a hairy werewolf mask. Nancy recognized Kevin Garcia's voice as he told monster jokes. . . .

"What's a werewolf's favorite bedtime story?" Kevin asked. "A hairy-tale!"

Kevin threw back his head and howled, "Ah-woooo!"

Nancy wasn't surprised to see their friend Nadine auditioning for *Twinkling Little Stars* too. She was the best dancer and actress in Ms. Ramirez's third-grade class.

"Is that a spider costume you're hanging up, Nadine?" Nancy asked.

"Not just any spider," Nadine said. She turned to three other kids hanging up the same costumes. "We're Cirque du Crawl-ay and we're dancing with a giant spider web!"

"Break a leg, Nadine," George said. "All eight of them!"

Across the room a small crowd was watching

Antonio Elefano, dressed as a vampire. The girls traded smirks. If Nadine was the class actress—Antonio was the class pest!

"Tell me, Mr. Fang," Antonio asked a bat puppet on his hand, "what is a vampire's favorite snack?"

Antonio used his other hand to lift a glass of grape juice to his lips. While he gulped it down the puppet said, "Scream of tomato, Count Joke-ula. Yum!"

"Pretty neat," Bess admitted. "How did he do that?"

"I don't know," Nancy admitted, "Since when is Antonio such a good ventriloquist?"

Suddenly George pointed to the floor underneath Antonio's long cape. "Hey!" she said. "Since when do vampires—have four feet?"

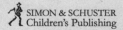

Code your Robot Puppy to Help Nancy Drew Solve the Mystery!

Nancy Drew: Codes & Clues introduces girls (5-8), to the basic concepts of coding while solving a fun mystery adventure game.

NANCY DREW AND THE CLUE CREW®
Test your detective skills with more Clue Crew cases!

Visit NancyDrew.com for the inside scoop!

From Aladdin · KIDS.SimonandSchuster.com

FOLLOW THE TRAIL AND SOLVE MYSTERIES WITH FRANK AND JOE!

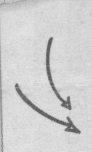

HardyBoysSeries.com